JE
MOS

3 2148 00125 9687

W9-AVM-314

Jungle Song

Miriam Moss
Illustrated by **Adrienne Kennaway**

5/05

FRANCES LINCOLN CHILDREN'S BOOKS

Early one morning a single fat raindrop slid off
a glossy green leaf high up in the trees. It fell through
the jungle air and landed with a plop on the nose
of a small sleeping tapir.

Little Tapir uncurled and looked up. Overhead hung
a spider as big as a bird.

"Follow me," whispered the spider silkily,
"and I will show you wonders you have never seen."

Spider led Tapir far away, away from his mother
where he should have stayed. But Tapir
was happy as he trotted along, because
in the beat of his feet he heard the jungle's song...

Deep in the jungle where cathedral trees
Rise like pillars with flickering leaves.
From the break of day in the cool half-light,
The jungle sings all through the night.

A howler monkey with a red-tipped tail,
Yells at Tapir – a piercing wail.
A bright blue butterfly, big as a hand,
Folds its wings as it drops to land.

There's a scraping sound and a long claw mark
As an anteater snuffles in crumbling bark.
A flycatcher shakes his feathers free,
While ants break open the root of a tree.

Spider points out for Tapir to see
The opening petals on the glow-fire tree.
The sun slides in, the day grows warm,
But Spider slips away before the storm.

The rain beats down in a thrumming roar,
Drumming out a pattern on the jungle floor.
A dead-eyed, heavy-weight anaconda
Uncoils herself to the sound of thunder.

Tapir hides to watch a snake
Glide and slide in the emerald lake,
And a lazy lizard with gold-green skin
Counts the ripples as a fly falls in.

The jungle drips and the river swirls along.
The swish and the swell is the river's song.
The flickering fish dart here and there,
Or leap and fly in the mist-filled air.

A termite army on the jungle floor
Marches out, driving all before.
A hercules beetle hides under leaves
And the air bursts open with the hum of bees.

Tapir tracks a line of leaf-cutter ants
Scissoring their way through the jungle plants.
And a cruising hornet up on high
Dangles its legs as it buzzes by.

Tapir spots a hummingbird, wings a-blur,
Hovering neatly, a whispering whirr.
There's a tap-tap strike of beak upon bark
As a woodpecker drums while it grows dark.

In the depths of dusk the sloth snores on
While the frog and toad beat out their song.
There's the drum of hoof and the pad, pad, pad
As the panther prowls dark velvet clad.

A treefrog clings with swollen toes.
A bullfrog croaks as the first star glows.
His bubble gum throat throws out a tune
As a spider spins silk beneath the moon.

A long-nosed bat laps nightly nectar,
Hanging upside down like a leather umbrella.
Hooting owl monkeys now roam free
Having hidden all day in the canopy.

Tapir's heart sings with his trotting feet,
But then he stops, he's missed the beat.

He sniffs, and senses something's wrong.
It's very dark and the song has gone.

Suddenly Tapir feels very tired...
all alone... and scared.

Just then a nose appears and a smooth
round neck.
   "There you are!" cries his mother.
"Thank goodness you're safe."
   She nuzzles Little Tapir and together
they disappear into the dark undergrowth.

So back they go, where cathedral trees
Rise like pillars with flickering leaves.
From the break of day in the cool half-light,
The jungle sings all through the night.

And Tapir is happy as they trot along
Because the beat of his feet IS the jungle's song.

About the Jungle

There are jungles in many parts of the world – in Central and South America, Africa, India and Southeast Asia. The jungle in this book is in South America. Jungles are also called *tropical rainforests*. This is because they are found in tropical areas where it rains a lot. The sun beats down strongly from almost overhead, every day of the year. Tropical rainforests are therefore very hot and humid, and are wonderful places for trees to grow.

Tapirs are just one of the multitude of amazing animals that live amongst the giant trees of the tropical forests. These trees can soar to over 50 metres (over 160 feet) in height – taller than a tower block. In fact, tropical rainforests contain more sorts of animals and plants than any other part of the earth.

Many plants from the tropical forests are the source of some of our foods and medicines. For example, bananas, pineapples, sugar cane and coffee were originally plants found in the rainforest.

Tropical forests are also very important because they affect what the weather does. Tropical forest trees draw up water that evaporates into the air to form clouds. Forests also help to protect soil from being washed away. As you can see, tropical forests are very important places, not just for the animals, but for us too.

David Bellamy